YOU CAN'T STOP THE
BIG BAD
BOGEY

C334403540

First published in 2019 by Scholastic Children's Books
Euston House, 24 Eversholt Street, London NW1 1DB
a division of Scholastic Ltd
www.scholastic.co.uk

London ~ New York ~ Toronto
Sydney ~ Auckland ~ Mexico City
New Delhi ~ Hong Kong

Printed in Malaysia
10 8 6 4 2 1 3 5 7 9

Papers used by Scholastic Children's Books are
made from wood grown in sustainable forests.

To Finn with love from

tim

For Annemieke and
Emma – partners in
mischief since 1977

Tom

YOU CAN'T STOP THE BIG BAD BOGEY

TIMOTHY KNAPMAN

TOM KNIGHT

SCHOLASTIC

Once upon a time,
in a faraway land...
a massive dragon ate a bogey.
It wasn't any old bogey.

It was the **Big Bad Bogey**
- the naughtiest bogey in the world!

In the dragon's tummy, the **Big Bad Bogey** met a Good Little Bogey that the dragon had eaten for breakfast. The Good Little Bogey said,

"Please don't do anything naughty."

But the Big Bad Bogey went bouncing around,
tickling and twisting things, just to
show him. And the Big Bad Bogey sang,

"You can't stop the Big Bad Bogey,
the Big Bad Bogey, the Big Bad Bogey!
You can't stop the Big Bad Bogey
having all the fun in the world!"

...sent both bogeys flying out of her mouth in a fiery "BLERP!"

"I asked you nicely!" yelled the Good Little Bogey, as they shot – **frazzled** and **fizzling** – through the air.

"Ha ha!"

laughed the Big Bad Bogey, but his bottom was **boiling hot** so he sploshed down into...

THE UGLY DUCKLING'S POND

where the Ugly Duckling had just told everyone that, when he grew up, he was going to be a beautiful swan.

But instead, the Big Bad Bogey **squished** him flat with a **hissing sizzle**.

"What are *YOU* going to be when you grow up?" asked the other ducklings.

"Disgusting!"

said the Good Little Bogey.

"Ha ha!"

laughed the Big Bad Bogey, but he was all wet, so he went **bouncing** over to...

"Don't you DARE dry yourself on her lovely hair!" warned the Good Little Bogey.

"Ha ha!" laughed the Big Bad Bogey and he grabbed the Good Little Bogey and they both went **sliding** down it.

"Hey, handsome Prince! Aren't you going to climb up my hair?"

asked Rapunzel.

"Yuk!

Not now it's had bogeys in it!"

replied the Handsome Prince with a shudder.

"Look what you've done!" said the Good Little Bogey. But the Big Bad Bogey just went **bouncing** over to...

where the Wicked Queen was about to give Snow White the **poisoned** apple.

"That's **not** an apple!" said Snow White.

"No," snapped the Good Little Bogey. "It's a **very naughty** bogey!"

"**A talking bogey?**" shrieked the Wicked Queen and she ran away screaming.

"So who's going to **poison me now?**" said Snow White, crossly.

"It's a very important part of my **Story!**"

The Good Little Bogey
grabbed the Big Bad Bogey.

"You're not going to ruin
any more stories!" he said.

The Big Bad Bogey tried to
struggle free...

...and the two bogeys went **rolling** and **wrestling** through the forest.

They **smashed** up the Witch's gingerbread house...

...**knocked down** the giant beanstalk...

...and burst into a castle where the Big Bad Bogey **grabbed** Beast from Beauty and started **dancing** with him.

"**Oi!**" said Beauty.

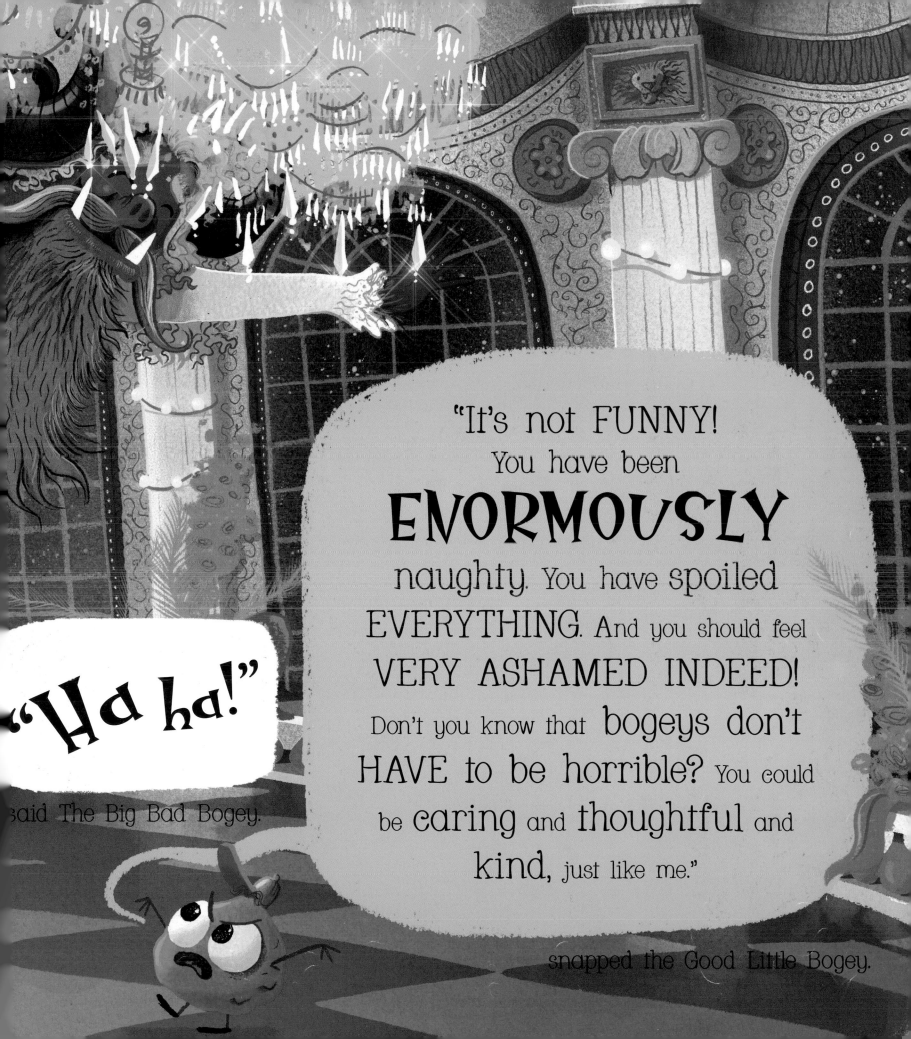

That made the Big Bad Bogey think.
Maybe, if he was caring and thoughtful and kind, the Good Little Bogey would be his friend.

Then they could play sweet games together...

...and eat neatly and make daisy chains...

...and sometimes even help old bogeys across the street.

There was just **one problem.**

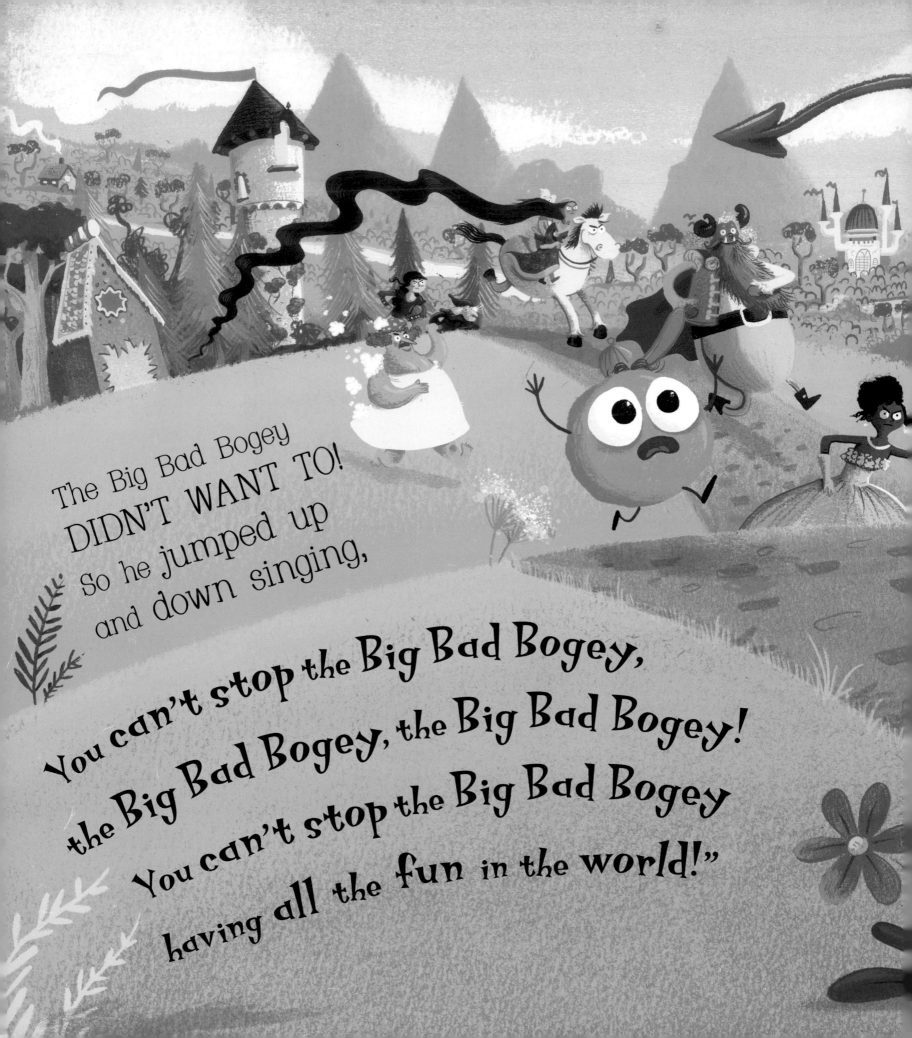

The Big Bad Bogey
DIDN'T WANT TO!
So he jumped up
and down singing,

You can't stop the Big Bad Bogey,
the Big Bad Bogey, the Big Bad Bogey!
You can't stop the Big Bad Bogey
having all the fun in the world!"

Then he **bounced off** to have billions more horrible adventures...

...because **nothing** could stop the Big Bad Bogey...

...well, nothing except being sat on by...

A BIG BAD BOTTOM!

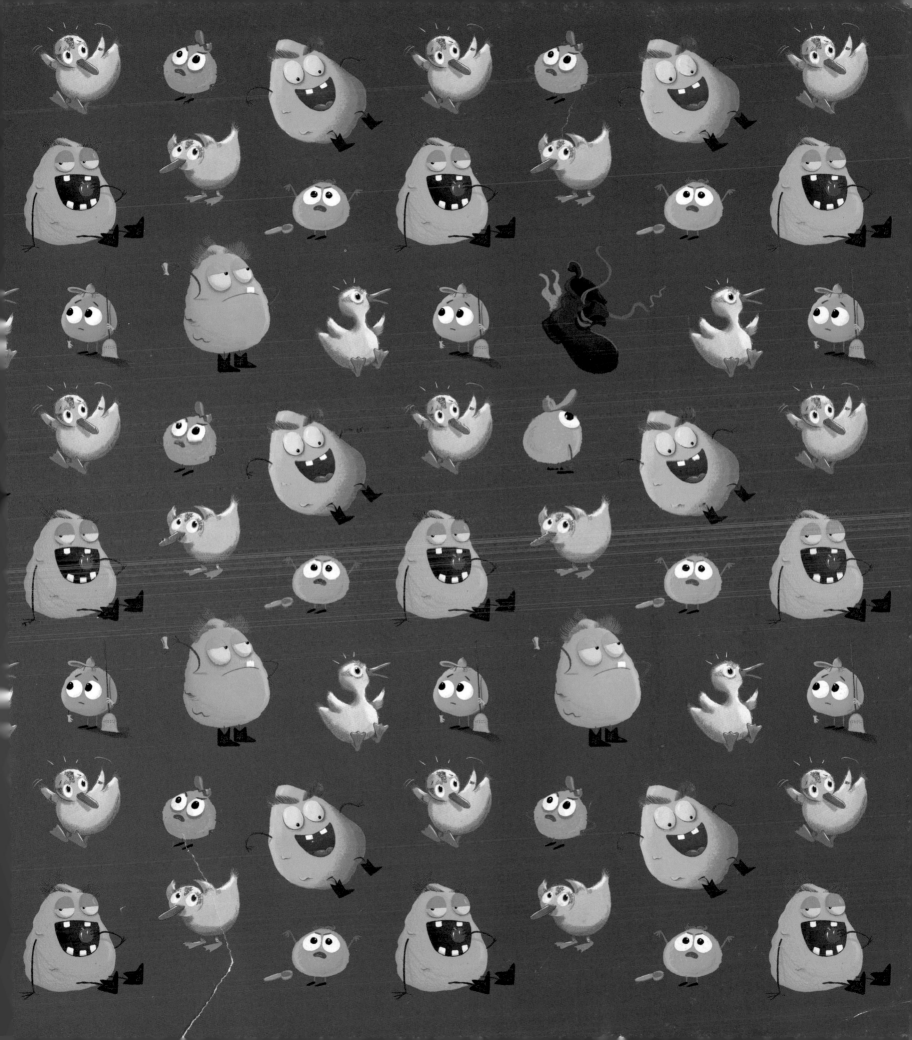